CODY AND QUINN, SITTING IN A TREE

CODY AND QUINN, SITTING IN A TREE

Kirby Larson

drawings by Nancy Poydar

Holiday House / New York

Library of Congress Cataloging-in-Publication Data
Larson, Kirby.
Cody and Quinn, sitting in a tree / Kirby Larson ; drawings by
Nancy Poydar. —1st ed.
p.   cm.
Summary: When the class bully teases him about his friendship with
a girl, Cody must decide whether to stay mad, to get even, or to
help his tormentor.
ISBN 0-8234-1227-X (alk. paper)
[1. Bullies—Fiction.   2. Schools—Fiction.   3. Friendship—
Fiction.]   I. Poydar, Nancy, ill.   II. Title.
PZ7.L32394Co   1996   95-25079   CIP   AC
[Fic]—dc20

For Donna and Dave
Miltenberger—loving parents,
cherished friends

K.L.

For Cody Minehart

N.P.

CODY AND QUINN, SITTING IN A TREE

CHAPTER ONE

"Mom, you're not doing it right." Cody Michaels slipped another package of Goody Cakes into his Amazing Man lunch box. "*That's* how I like my lunch."

"That's how I like mine, too," agreed his mother. Then she took out the second package of Goody Cakes. "What did the peel say to the banana?

"Don't move, I've got you covered." He watched Mom put a banana in his lunch box. Darn!

Cody bent down to tie his brand-new shoes. They were clean and white with two colors of purple stripes on the side. "All Royce brings for lunch is a bag of candy."

"Hmm." Mom added a drink to his lunch and closed the lid. "Better hurry. Quinn will leave without you." Cody and his friend Quinn Kelley walked to the bus stop together every day.

Cody grabbed his lunch box. The banana made it heavy.

"Goody Cakes are easier to carry," he said.

"Come give me a hug." Mom smooshed him. "This has to last until I get back from my late meeting tonight. Don't forget, Dad's got to take his paintings over to that new gallery, so Tyson will be here when you get home."

Tyson was Quinn's big brother. "That makes two good things—new shoes and Tyson!" Cody stopped for a second. "And one bad thing. The spelling test."

Mom smiled. "You'll do fine—you knew all the words last night."

Cody hurried out the door to Quinn's. Mom didn't understand that doing spelling words at home and taking a test at school were not the same thing. The minute Cody numbered his paper, the whole alphabet flew right out of his brain.

"Good morning, Cody!" Mrs. Kelley greeted his knock. "Quinn's running late. Come on in."

Cody followed her into the front hall. He liked the Kelleys' house. It always smelled like popcorn.

"I can't find my blue whale socks!" Quinn hollered down the stairs.

"Wear something else," Mrs. Kelley called back.

"*Mo-om!* Wednesday is spelling test day. I always wear my whale socks on spelling test days."

"These will have to do." Mrs. Kelley tossed up a pair of cat socks to Quinn.

Quinn fussed as she put them on. "Now we're probably going to miss the bus."

"Not if we run! Come on." Cody jogged a few steps in front of Quinn so she would notice his new shoes.

"I hate wearing the wrong socks for tests," Quinn grumbled as they ran down the street.

They made it in the nick of time. The bus had just turned up the block.

Cody bent down to brush some grass off his new shoes. He lifted up his right one to admire it. "Did you notice how fast I was running?" he asked. He bounced in place a few times.

Finally, Quinn looked down. "Oh, those are neat. They're just like Tyson's."

"Only smaller," said Cody.

"They probably smell lots better, too," said Quinn.

The school bus swooshed to a stop in front of them. Cody let Quinn get on first.

"Come on, let's sit here." Quinn slid onto the seat and Cody followed. Quinn usually saved a place every morning for her friend Manuela. But Manuela had the chicken pox and would be gone for the whole week.

Cody was careful not to kick his feet against the seat in front. That would make their driver, Dora the Dragon Lady, mad. Also, he didn't want to wreck his new shoes.

Quinn studied Cody's feet. "Maybe shoes can be lucky, too," she said. "They helped you run fast so we didn't miss the bus."

Cody sat up straight. His feet tingled inside his white and purple shoes. "Do you think they might work for spelling?"

Quinn shrugged then looked at her own feet. "Cats!" she said.

Cody turned his baseball cap around. "You know, upside down, those cats look kind of like whales."

Quinn squinted. "You think so?"

"A lot like whales."

Quinn tilted her head this way. Then

7

she tilted her head that way. "They do. Especially when you squint."

At the next bus stop, Annie May, Caitlin Murphy, and a bunch of other kids hopped on. The bus got noisier.

Royce Hendricks swaggered to the seat in front of Cody and Quinn. He opened a carton of Tastee Juice, even though it was against the bus rules.

"Sitting with your girlfriend again," said Royce, leaning over the back of his seat. "It must be true love!"

"Turn around, Royce," said Quinn.

"Make me," said Royce. Just then, the bus bounced over a pothole in the road. Cody and Quinn bumped and slid on their seat. Royce's Tastee Juice bounced out of his hand and onto the floor at Cody's feet.

Red juice splattered everywhere. Cody's new white and purple shoes looked like they had chicken pox, like Manuela.

"Oops!" Royce laughed.

Cody tried to wipe his shoes off on each

other. That just smeared the juice all around.

"I saw that, mister," called Dora from the driver's seat.

She looked at Cody through her big rear-view mirror. "No food or drink on the bus—you know that."

Cody felt his face get hot.

"Since you can't follow the rules, you better come sit here, behind me."

"But I didn't—"

Dora cut him off. "I'd hate to have to write you a behavior ticket," she said. "Now, pick up that box and come here."

"Can't you follow the rules?" asked Royce. He snickered as Cody bent over to pick up the empty Tastee Juice carton.

Glick, glick, glick. Cody's shoes felt like suction cups as he moved up the aisle. *Glick, glick.* He slid into the seat behind Dora.

He pulled his baseball cap over his face. His new shoes weren't lucky. They were yucky. Just like stupid old Royce.

CHAPTER TWO

At circle time, Cody sat on his feet so no one would see his stained shoes.

Royce sat behind Annie May. He tossed bits of paper at her head. Some of it stuck in her hair, like popcorn.

Clap-clappa-clap-clap went Mrs. Palmer's hands. *Clap-clap* answered the class.

"A change of plans, today," said Mrs. Palmer, when everyone was quiet. "Instead of spelling after circle time, we're going to do a special project."

Cody's ears perked up.

"*Yess!*" said Jim. "No spelling."

"At least, not until after lunch," said Mrs. Palmer. Then she emptied a bag of white socks on the rainbow worktable. "Everyone will need a partner for this project."

Cody looked over at Quinn. She nodded yes.

Royce had spread his Major Marvel cards out on the floor. "Oh, look, Cody wants to be with his girlfriend." He fanned a card under his chin.

"Some people are not following directions." Mrs. Palmer set down a plastic tub overflowing with bits of ribbon and lace and yarn. "Royce, those cards belong in your backpack."

"Mrs. Palmer," called Annie May. "I don't have a partner."

"Is there anyone else who needs one?" asked Mrs. Palmer.

Royce raised his hand.

"There, Annie May. You and Royce can work together."

13

"Not with a girl! No way." Royce folded his arms across his chest.

Annie May made snake eyes at him. "Why can't Cody and Royce be partners, then I could be with Quinn?"

Cody held his breath. Please, for once, don't let bossy old Annie May get her own way.

"Cody, do you want to switch partners?"

Cody shook his head.

"Quinn, do you?"

Quinn shook her head.

"You and Royce will be a great team, Annie May."

Both Annie May and Royce groaned.

Mrs. Palmer reached into her red Bag of Tricks. She pulled out her hand.

Brynn's arm shot up. "It's a Charlotte the spider puppet," she said. "Can I try it?"

Mrs. Palmer passed the Charlotte sock puppet around the circle for everyone to try.

"Can anyone guess what our project is?" Mrs. Palmer asked.

"A puppet show!" Caitlin called out.

Mrs. Palmer smiled. "Good guess, Caitlin, but remember to raise your hand."

Jim raised his hand. "Do we get to make our own puppets?"

"Yes," said Mrs. Palmer. "And you can act out any story you and your partner agree on."

"How long do we have?" asked Brynn.

"Friday will be puppet show day. So you have three days, counting today. Any other questions?" She pointed. "Annie May?"

"I have a real puppet at home," Annie May bragged.

"Perhaps you could bring it for sharing," said Mrs. Palmer.

Cody and Quinn walked over to the rainbow worktable. Cody's shoes were only a little bit sticky now. He picked up a sock and tried wiping off some of the juice spots.

"Which story should we do?" asked Quinn. She tied a lace scrap in her hair.

Cody shrugged. He spit on the sock and wiped again. That helped.

"I know what you should do," said Royce, making goo-goo eyes at them.

Quinn glared. "Tick-a-lock, Royce."

"What does that mean?" he asked.

"Wouldn't you like to know?" Quinn tossed her head.

"Royce, you're not helping," said Annie May. "Mrs. Palmer!"

"What *does* 'tick-a-lock' mean?" Cody whispered to Quinn.

Quinn glanced over her shoulder. Royce was now sock fighting with Philip. She leaned closer to Cody. "Mom doesn't let me say shut up anymore. So I say tick-a-lock instead."

"I like it!" Cody tried it out. "Tick-a-lock. Tick-a-lock."

"So, what story?" Quinn glanced over at the class bookcase. "How about—"

"Ouch!" Cody whirled around.

"I know what story you should do!"

Royce danced around Cody, flicking him again and again on the arm with the sock.

"Mrs. Palmer!" called Quinn.

"Royce!" Mrs. Palmer came over and took away Royce's sock.

"*Sleeping Beauty!* Smooch Smooch!" Royce blew kisses everywhere.

Mrs. Palmer pointed to the time-out chair in the quiet reading corner. Royce sat.

"Try to ignore him," Mrs. Palmer said to Quinn and Cody as they returned to their seats.

Cody picked up a pencil and began to doodle on his desk. He liked making squiggles and then turning them into something. This squiggle was turning into Amazing Man. He had wrapped a big rope around his archenemy, The Hook. Cody added an *A* to Amazing Man's cape.

"What about *Amazing Man's Adventures*?" he said.

Quinn wrinkled her nose.

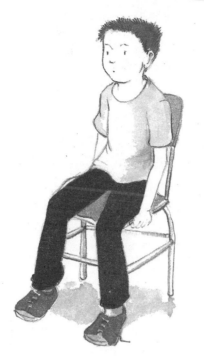

"Then how about *Miss Nelson is Missing?*"

"Annie May'll do that one. It's her favorite." Quinn flipped her ponytail over her head and peered out at Cody through fringes of brown hair. "I know—*George and Martha!*"

19

"*Yess!*" Cody jumped up in excitement. "I'll make George and you make Martha." They hurried back to the rainbow worktable, rummaged through the scrap tub and brought back fistfuls of scraps.

Royce wandered by, humming "Here Comes the Bride."

Cody covered his ears.

"Go jump in a lake, Royce," said Quinn.

Royce waltzed away, humming even louder.

Cody picked up his pencil again. The Hook had discovered Amazing Man's weakness. From his secret Hook-sleeve, he pulled out a pouch of Gazorkium. Amazing Man fell to his knees, clutching his stomach.

Cody's stomach didn't feel so great either, especially right now with Royce making disgusting smooching noises every time he went past.

"Oh, listen, I hear an ape somewhere," Quinn said very loudly, looking straight at

Royce. "It must have escaped from the zoo."

Royce's cheeks got as red as cherry drops. He made an ugly face at Quinn.

She turned her back to him.

Quinn was brave to stand up to Royce. Cody was brave, too, when it came to the monkey bars and skateboarding, but not when it came to Royce.

Royce squinted at Cody. "I'm going to tell that you're drawing on your desk."

Cody licked his thumb and smeared his picture. All that was left was the *A* on Amazing Man's cape. Cody let out a deep, discouraged breath.

"Royce, get over here and help," ordered Annie May.

Mrs. Palmer put her hands on Royce's shoulders and guided him to where Annie May was working.

One more swipe of the thumb rubbed off the last of Amazing Man.

"You know, there are a lot of George and Martha stories," said Quinn. "Which one shall we pick?" They talked about their favorites.

"My best story is the one where George brags about diving from the high dive and gets too scared," started Quinn.

"Yeah, so Martha dives off and makes such a huge splash that George can climb down without anyone seeing," finished Cody. "I like that one, too."

Kids in the front of the room were getting very noisy. Lots of them were laughing. Cody looked up and saw that someone had drawn a huge red heart on the white board. The initials inside were C.M. and Q.K.

Cody ran up and erased as fast as he could. Now, everyone was laughing and pointing.

"Quiet voices, class!" Mrs. Palmer clapped her hands. Kids were being so loud and noisy no one clapped back. "Class!" she said again.

Royce was laughing so hard, you could

see his tonsils. Cody wanted to throw the eraser right at his big mouth.

Mrs. Palmer flicked the lights. "Heads down. Zero noise for one minute."

Cody dropped the eraser. If Amazing Man were here he'd—

"Cody, that means you, too," said Mrs. Palmer.

Cody hurried to his seat and ducked his head down. Royce Hendricks was worse than Gazorkium. Ten times worse.

CHAPTER THREE

As soon as the recess bell rang, Cody ran outside, straight for the monkey bars and far away from Royce. Cody had taught himself how to do a bird's nest and a waterfall. Now, he wanted to learn to do a freaky Friday. It was hard to turn himself all the way around on the bar. His hands kept slipping.

Cody took a deep breath. He kicked his feet hard and hung on tight. He did it!

"That was great!" cried Quinn. She climbed up next to him.

Cody felt just like he did when he learned to ride his bike without training wheels. "Wow. I'm going to do it again!" He did. Again and again.

"You better take a break," Quinn warned. "Remember that time Brynn did twenty-five freaky Fridays in a row, and then she threw up?"

Cody did feel a little queasy.

"I thought you were playing four square," he said.

"I was." Quinn hung from her knees. "Royce called a liner so I was out."

"He's a banana brain," said Cody. "I wish he'd shut—I mean, tick-a-lock."

Quinn swung back and forth. "Just ignore him."

Cody adjusted his baseball cap. Quinn was used to teasing. Tyson bugged her all the time. Cody didn't have any brothers or sisters to bug him. If he did, maybe he wouldn't have such a hard time with Royce.

"Oh, look, here are the lovebirds!" Royce

ran over and climbed up on the bars with them. He punched Cody on the shoulder. "Have you asked her to go out yet?"

"Tick-a-lock," said Quinn. She did a roll over the middle bar.

"Yeah," said Cody. He did another bird's nest to show he didn't care about Royce.

"That's so easy." Royce swung up on the bar next to Cody. "Even my little sister can do that."

Cody did another bird's nest.

"The bars are for babies." Royce sneered at Cody.

"No, they're not. My uncle Jess does the bars and he's in college." Cody flipped himself right side up. "He might get to be in the Olympics."

Royce didn't say anything, just wrapped his knees around the bar and hung upside down. He tried to do a waterfall. And landed on his bottom. "Ouch!"

Cody couldn't help laughing. Royce looked kind of funny, the way he landed.

Like a bundle of Royce rags. Quinn giggled, too.

Royce stood up. His voice got loud. "Why do you do whatever your boyfriend does?" he asked.

Annie May and some other kids came over.

"Cody and Quinn, sitting in a tree . . ." taunted Royce.

Cody plugged his ears.

". . . *k-i-s-s-i-n-g*." Royce wagged his face in front of Cody.

Cody jumped down off the bars. "Stop it. I mean it."

"It's a free country, isn't it?" said Royce. "I can say anything I want."

Royce danced around, poking at Cody. Cody's chest felt like an elephant was standing on it.

"Knock it off." Cody brushed Royce's hand away.

"First comes love, then comes marriage—" Royce sang. He wouldn't stop.

"I don't love her," Cody screamed. His

heart pounded like a hammer on his ribs.
"I hate her!"

Before he ran away, Cody saw Quinn's
face. She looked like she'd had the wind
knocked out of her.

He knew exactly how she felt.

CHAPTER FOUR

Cody was the last one in from recess. He trudged to his seat, pulling his cap over his face so no one could see him.

As he sat down, Mrs. Palmer told them to take out a piece of paper. "Please number your papers one through twelve," she said.

Cody picked up his pencil but wasn't sure he could even remember how to spell his own name. By the time the test was over, his paper looked like Swiss cheese, full of holes from erasing so hard.

"Now, trade with the person across from you for correcting," said Mrs. Palmer. She switched on the overhead projector.

Cody slid his paper over to Quinn. She flipped hers back at him without even looking up.

"The first word is *ocean*," said Mrs. Palmer. "*O-c-e a-n*."

Quinn had spelled it right. Cody made a blue smiley face next to the number one on her paper. He wished he could remember how he'd spelled ocean. He thought he spelled it right. Mostly.

By the time Mrs. Palmer reached the last word, Cody had drawn twelve smiley faces on Quinn's test.

"I guess your cat socks were lucky for spelling, after all!" Cody said. Quinn didn't answer. She had her arm across Cody's paper and was writing something at the top. With her red pencil.

"When you're finished, hand the papers back." Mrs. Palmer turned off the overhead projector.

Cody pushed Quinn's test toward her side of the table, then pulled it back and wrote "grate werk" at the top, like Mrs. Palmer sometimes did.

Quinn tossed his test back. Not one word had a smiley face by it. Heavy red check marks squatted next to each number.

"Pretty soon, you're going to have to go to Mr. Grumman's class," Quinn said.

Cody didn't want to be one of Grummie's Dummies. He tried to swallow but it felt like a wad of bubblegum was stuck in his throat. Usually, when Quinn corrected his spelling papers, she wrote things like "good try," even if he missed a lot.

He knew he had hurt her feelings out on the playground. But it wasn't his fault! Royce shouldn't have teased him so much. Quinn should know he didn't hate her.

They'd been good friends since they were babies!

Cody got an idea. He nudged Quinn to get her attention. "Hey, do you want to go to the fort after school? I'll bring some Goody Cakes."

Before she could answer, Royce butted

in. "Oh, Cody and Quinn are going to play house after school. Isn't that sweet?"

Cody counted to five. Ignore Royce. Ignore Royce.

"Quinn, do you want to?"

"Cody plus Quinn equals true love," mooed Royce.

Cody's ears tingled.

"Tick-a-lock, Royce," Quinn shouted.

"Quinn!" Mrs. Palmer sounded surprised.

Quinn buried her face in her arms. She kept her head down on the desk for a long time.

It was all Royce's fault. There had to be some way to make him stop. But how?

Cody began to doodle on his spelling test. Soon, Amazing Man appeared on the paper. Things looked bad for him. The Hook had him trapped in a cage. He was turning a crank to lower Amazing Man into a pit of, of—

Something stung Cody on the back of the neck. A spitwad. Royce!

Cody looked down at his drawing. Scorpions. That's what Amazing Man was being dropped into. A pit of scorpions.

CHAPTER FIVE

"Quinn, wait up!" Cody called after school, but Quinn ran ahead as if she were trying to escape a monster. Even with his new shoes, Cody couldn't catch her.

He wished his parents were going to be home. Mom would cheer him up with one of her dumb jokes. The one yesterday was: What does the little gnome do when he gets home from school? Gnomework. Or Dad might take him to the park so they could sketch with Cody's new sketch pad and maybe shoot some hoops.

But Dad was at the art gallery and Mom was at that meeting. Cody opened the back door and went straight to the kitchen. A snack would help. There were still those Goody Cakes Mom took out of his lunch.

"I'm home, Tyson," Cody called out. He poured himself some apple juice. He rummaged in the cupboard. Where were those Goody Cakes?

Tyson wandered into the room. He had an empty wrapper in his hand. He threw it in the garbage.

"Those were *my* Goody Cakes!" Cody said.

"Sorry about that," Tyson said. "How about a banana instead?"

Cody left the apple juice on the table and went back to his bedroom. He picked up a black pencil and scribbled hard dark lines on his drawing pad. It looked like a thunder and lightning storm.

"Knock, knock." Tyson stood in the

doorway. "I brought my baseball cards over. Want to help me organize them?"

Cody added some more zigzags of lightning to his picture.

"Wow," said Tyson. "You're going to be a good artist. Just like your dad." He leaned over Cody's shoulder. "When you're done here, I could sure use your help." Tyson wandered back to the family room.

Cody bent over his desk, sketching and erasing. Nothing was turning out right, not even when he tried to draw Amazing Man.

He crumpled up his drawing paper and went to look for Tyson. "I guess I could help for a little while."

Tyson pushed a shoe box toward Cody. "Go through these. Pull out all the Mariners cards and put them in that blue box, there."

If Cody had a big brother, he would want him to be like Tyson. Even if he did eat other people's Goody Cakes. Tyson knew all the sports teams and players. He made

39

the world's best peanut butter chocolate chip cookies. And he was big. Bigger than Royce.

Cody stretched out on the floor. He wished Tyson went to their school, instead of Southshore Junior High.

"Hey, what happened to your shoes?" Tyson asked.

Cody tried to sit on his feet. "Nothing."

"Nothing?" asked Tyson. "It looks like you were attacked by some mutant strawberries!"

Cody studied a Ken Griffey, Jr. baseball card. "Some juice got spilled on them." Tyson looked so concerned that Cody told him what had happened.

Tyson checked something off on his clipboard. "That Royce is a twerp."

"Twerp." Cody nodded his head.

"Are you going to let him get away with stuff like that?"

Cody shrugged. "I don't know. I don't like it."

"There are two ways to deal with someone like Royce," said Tyson.

"There are?" Cody stopped flipping through cards.

Tyson blew a bubble. "You bet. You either get mad or you get even."

Cody thought about that. He was already mad at Royce. And that sure hadn't done anything. Maybe he needed to get even.

Tyson unwrapped another piece of gum and popped it into his mouth. He offered Cody a piece, too. "Let him have it—*Pow!*"

Cody unwrapped the bubblegum. He chewed it noisily while he flipped through another box of baseball cards. *Pow!* He snapped the gum. Then Royce would leave him alone.

He blew a huge bubble. Tyson popped it.

"Come on," he said. "I'm tired of this. Let's go make some cookies."

"Okay!" said Cody. Tonight was lasagna

night. Those big, slimy noodles always got jammed in his throat. If they made cookies, Cody might get too full for lasagna. Tyson was loaded with good ideas. Cody punched at the air with his fist.

Pow!

Better watch out, Royce.

CHAPTER SIX

Cody ran over to Quinn's the next morning.

"She just left," said Mrs. Kelley. "I thought she'd gone over to get you."

As he walked down the block, Cody could see Quinn leaning against the bus stop sign. She had her back to him.

"Hi, Quinn," he called when he got closer.

She didn't answer.

"Hi, Quinn," he called louder.

No answer.

He was close enough now to see she was wearing earmuffs. Even though the daffodils were blooming and the spring sun was shining.

When the bus pulled up, Quinn hurried on. She stretched her legs across the seat so Cody couldn't sit with her.

At the next stop, Tiffany slid onto the seat with Quinn; Annie May and Caitlin sat behind them. They put their heads together and whispered. Cody couldn't hear them. But, every so often, they'd turn their heads back and look at him.

Royce had gotten on, too, and was trading Major Marvel cards with a third grader.

Thwinnng. Cody rubbed his cheek. *Thwinnng.* More spitwads! He heard Royce laughing. Of course, Dora the Dragon Lady didn't even notice. Cody slumped down in his seat and pulled his baseball cap over his face. Just wait, Royce. Pretty soon it'll be *Pow*-time!

At school, Annie May got off first, carry-

45

ing a small suitcase. She hurried to show Mrs. Palmer what was inside.

"It's a marionette," she said in her know-it-all voice. "My grandma brought it from Italy."

Cody put his fingers in his ears but he could still hear Annie May blah-blah-blahing.

"Let me try it." Royce picked up the handles of the fancy puppet.

"You'll wreck it!" screeched Annie May. She jerked it out of Royce's hands.

"No, I won't." As they wrestled, Royce's backpack slipped off and something fell out. His Major Marvel cards. They landed near Mrs. Palmer's bookcase.

"Annie May, perhaps you better put the marionette by your desk until sharing time." Mrs. Palmer helped Annie May put the fancy puppet back in the suitcase. Cody held his breath. No one said anything about the cards. Not Mrs. Palmer. Not Annie May. Not Royce.

It was time to get even!

Moving slowly, Cody walked to the front of the room. Royce had followed Annie May back to her desk. "Puppets are for girls, anyway," he said.

Cody was right next to the cards. He stretched his foot out.

"Royce, please put your backpack in the coat room." Mrs. Palmer turned to check the lunch count.

Just . . . a . . . little . . . bit . . . farther. Cody flicked his foot. There! The Major Marvel cards disappeared under the bookcase. *Pow!* Take that, Royce!

"Cody, please come join us in the calendar corner."

Cody jumped at Mrs. Palmer's voice. He rushed over and sat down on the circle rug next to Josh. He sneaked a peek over at the bookcase. It seemed like the cards gave off a glow that no one else saw.

All morning, Cody's attention kept wandering over to the bookcase. When he went to sharpen his pencil before spelling, he double-checked whether anybody could see the cards poking out. They were absolutely hidden. Now, he just had to wait until Royce noticed they were missing.

He only had to wait until lunchtime. "Hey," hollered Royce as he pawed through his backpack. "Where are my new Major Marvel cards?"

Cody unwrapped his bologna and ketchup sandwich. He took a bite and chewed slowly.

Royce dumped everything out of his desk. "All right. Who took my cards?"

Mrs. Palmer helped sort through the mess on the floor. She handed Royce a library book. "This was due three weeks ago."

Royce pushed the book back in his desk. Mrs. Palmer pulled it out again.

"Someone took my cards. I know it." Royce glared around the room. "Who's got them?"

Cody studied the side of his milk carton.

"Jim—did you?" Royce grabbed Jim's arm.

"No way. I hate Major Marvel cards."
Jim shook off Royce's hand.

"Royce." Mrs. Palmer's voice was firm.
"That's not the way to handle this."

Cody wiggled in his seat.

Mrs. Palmer folded her arms. "Are you
positive you brought them to school?"

"I saw them on the bus," said Tiffany. "I

50

know, because I was going to trade him my Turtle Boy for the Hawk Woman."

"No deal," said Royce. "I have five Turtle Boys at home."

Mrs. Palmer cleared her throat. "Has anyone seen Royce's cards?"

Cody picked up a pencil. Amazing Man appeared once again on his desk. Amazing Man was finally getting even with his archenemy, The Hook. Amazing Man knew where The Hook's secret power pack was and The Hook didn't. Amazing Man was never going to tell The Hook. Amazing Man had a big smile.

So did Cody.

CHAPTER SEVEN

After lunch recess, Cody glanced over at the bookcase. He wondered if he should make sure the cards were still there. He looked over his left shoulder. Annie May was busy bossing some of the girls around. Mrs. Palmer was helping Jim and Josh with math. All clear.

Cody walked over, slowly. Then he dropped to his knees, pretending to look for his pencil. He peeked under the bookcase. There they were. Good.

When he stood up, he noticed Quinn watching him. She gave him a funny look. He turned quickly and hurried back to his seat.

Then, Quinn walked over to sharpen her pencil. On her way back, she dropped it. Right by the bookcase.

Cody's legs felt as wobbly as if he'd ridden his bike for twenty miles.

Quinn was down on her hands and knees. She fished around under the bookcase. Then she stood, holding something up in her hand.

"Hey, my cards!" Royce blurted out. "How'd they get there?"

"I bet they fell out when your backpack slipped off this morning," said Mrs. Palmer. "Sharp eyes, Quinn."

Quinn didn't say anything. She gave Cody the kind of look Mom gave him when she asked if he'd really brushed his teeth before bed.

Cody sunk down in his chair. Was

Quinn going to tell on him? She was mad enough to.

"Now, Royce, please put these in your backpack." Mrs. Palmer handed him the cards.

Quinn returned to her seat. Cody let out his breath.

Mrs. Palmer sat in her rocker. "Let's do our sharing now. I see that Caitlin and Brynn have signed up."

"Me, too!" called out Annie May. "I have my special you-know-what."

"You may share next, Annie May."

Caitlin and Brynn walked to the front of the room.

"We're doing a science experiment," said Brynn. She giggled.

"Making volcanoes," added Caitlin.

"Wow!" said Josh. "Run for your lives!"

Cody sat up straighter. Volcanoes were interesting! Way better than Annie May's dumb old marionette.

"This is a very small volcano," said Brynn. "Watch closely."

They put two jars on the table. Brynn shook some white powder from one jar into a bowl. "Baking soda," she said, importantly.

Caitlin opened her jar. It was filled with liquid.

"It smells like pickles!" said Quinn.

"I think so, too," said Cody. Quinn just sniffed and turned her head away.

"Vinegar," said Caitlin, pouring it into the bowl.

Suddenly, white foam gushed over the edge of the bowl.

"*Ye-ow*," said Josh. "It really works!"

"My turn," said Annie May.

"Thanks, girls." Mrs. Palmer helped Brynn and Caitlin clean up. "That was fun. Maybe tomorrow we can talk about why the vinegar makes the baking soda foam up like that."

Annie May grabbed her suitcase and bustled up to the front of the room. The marionette was colorful but Cody's mind wandered as soon as Annie May started talking. He was thinking about the volcano experiment and about Royce. It seemed like everyone in the class was like the baking soda, except Royce. He was the vinegar. Whenever you added him to anything, there was an explosion.

"Cody, you need to pay attention." Mrs. Palmer stood by his desk. "Sharing is over now. It's time to work on your puppet plays." Cody got out his George puppet. He'd done a good job but it still needed something.

"Quinn, do you think there's something missing from my puppet?" he asked.

"Do you hear anything, Caitlin?" Quinn asked.

"No, nothing," Caitlin answered with a giggle.

"That's what I thought." Quinn flipped her head, ponytail swishing.

She still wasn't speaking to him. Which was going to make it very hard to do the puppet show. They hadn't practiced once and tomorrow was puppet show day!

"That is the ugliest puppet I've ever seen," Annie May was saying to Royce. His puppet did look more like a slug than a person. "It doesn't even look like Miss Nelson. Can't you do anything right? Why did I have to get stuck with you! Mrs. Palmer!" Annie May went running over to the teacher.

Tiffany came over. "Cody, can you draw the eyes on for me? I can't get them right."

Cody took his marker and drew two cow eyes on Tiffany's Ferdinand puppet. "Take a look at this." He showed her his George puppet. "Does it look all right to you?"

Tiffany chewed her lower lip. "It looks fine to me," she said. "You're so good at art." Just as she handed the puppet back to Cody, another hand reached in and snatched it away.

"Give it back!"

"Oh, Quinn-Martha," Royce made the George puppet say. "Will you marry me?"

"Tick-a-lock, Royce." Cody made a swipe for the puppet.

"Here comes the groom," sang Royce as he twirled this way and that.

Cody zigged and zagged as he tried to rescue George.

"Royce, Cody! What's going on?" Mrs. Palmer marched toward them.

Royce froze. Cody grabbed the puppet and pulled. Royce hung on. George's right ear came off.

"Hey!" hollered Cody.

"Boys!" Mrs. Palmer's voice was as sharp as broken glass.

Royce threw the puppet. Before Cody could catch it, it landed in the bussing tray from lunch. Cody picked George out of the corn niblets and leftover tater tots.

"Too bad, Cody. Now Martha will have to find another boyfriend." Royce made a fake sad face.

Mrs. Palmer put her hand on Cody's shoulder.

He was sure she could feel the mad boiling and bubbling inside his skin.

"Royce, down to Mrs. Moore's office.

Now." Cody had never heard Mrs. Palmer sound so cross.

"I didn't do anything," said Royce. "Cody tripped me and I dropped his puppet. It was an accident."

Cody felt Mrs. Palmer's fingers grip his shoulder a little tighter. "Royce, do as you are told."

When he passed in front of Cody, Royce stopped. "It was a stupid puppet anyway. It didn't even look like George. Where was his gold tooth?"

That did it. Cody swung his clenched fist. *Pow!*

"Owww!" bellowed Royce, holding his stomach.

"Cody!" cried Mrs. Palmer.

"Oh, tick-a-lock," said Cody.

CHAPTER EIGHT

The principal, Mrs. Moore, reached into her jacket pocket and pulled out a packet of peanut butter crackers. She was always munching on something. She offered one to Cody. He loved peanut butter crackers but his mouth was so dry he was afraid he'd choke to death.

"Why don't you tell me what happened?" she asked. "I've already talked to Royce."

Cody looked at Mrs. Moore through his watery eyes. She had a friendly face. But it would be too hard to explain. He shook his head and sniffled.

"Hmm." Mrs. Moore ate another cracker. "Want to hear about something that happened to me?" She brushed crumbs off her shirt. "When I was in grade school, there was this girl who bugged me all the time. She called me Dumbo and made fun of my ears." Mrs. Moore pulled her hair back. Her ears did stick out. "She kept bugging me until one day I couldn't take it anymore. Do you know what I did?"

Cody swung his legs, back and forth. He had a hard time picturing Mrs. Moore as a little girl.

"I cut off one of her pigtails." Mrs. Moore smiled in a sad sort of way.

"You did?" Cody stopped swinging his legs.

"Yep. And, boy, did I get in big trouble.

The principal called my mom and she had to come to school. They made me pay for the girl to get a haircut to even out her hair."

"Did the girl stop teasing you?"

Mrs. Moore reached for another cracker, then stopped. "Actually, she moved away."

Cody sighed. Just when it was beginning to get interesting, too. Oh, well. Royce didn't have pigtails anyway.

"The point is, that getting even—whether it's cutting off pigtails or punching someone—isn't a very good choice. I know you can make good choices, Cody. See what you can figure out." She stood up and walked around her desk to open the door.

Cody walked like a turtle back to Room three. He snuck into his seat and pulled his baseball cap down so Quinn couldn't see his face.

Royce was slouched at his desk, reading a library book. Cody waited for him to say something mean. But he didn't take his eyes off the book.

Cody pulled out his own library book and started reading. Out of the corner of his eye he saw something he couldn't believe.

A big tear fell—*Plop*—right onto Royce's book.

Cody sat back. He peeked over again. *Plop!* Another tear.

A funny feeling came over Cody. He tugged on his baseball cap. Maybe, just maybe, Royce didn't like being the vinegar all the time.

CHAPTER NINE

"Hi, Cody!" Mom was doing some paper-work on the kitchen table when he got home from school. "I've got a new one for you today," she said. "Which traffic light is the bravest?"

Cody dropped his backpack with a thud.

"Give up already?" Mom teased. "The one that doesn't turn yellow!"

Cody couldn't even fake a smile.

"How about a snack?" asked Mom. She opened the cupboard and pulled out a package of Goody Cakes. "Do you want to take this out to the fort?"

"Maybe later." Cody slumped into the chair next to Mom.

"What's the trouble, bubble?" Mom asked.

Cody blew out a big breath. He dug the ruined George puppet out of his backpack.

"Looks like George had a catastrophe," Mom said, taking the puppet out of Cody's hand. "Is this what's the matter?"

Cody felt like a lump of cold mashed potatoes. "One of the things," he said.

"Do you want to try to fix this?" Mom asked.

Cody shook his head. "No, I better start over." He wished you could start over with friends like you could with puppets.

"Do you want some help?"

"Naw. I can do it." Cody wandered off to find some fabric scraps. Mrs. Palmer had already given him another sock. He started to work.

Mom peeked in on him a little while

later. "Hey, that looks great! Even better than your first one."

"You really think so?" Cody asked, examining the puppet from every angle.

"Yes, I do."

It was a good George puppet. Cody had made him some flowered swim trunks and a blue striped shirt. And a gold tooth.

"Maybe I will have those Goody Cakes," he said, feeling better than he had in a long time. "Maybe I should take a package for George, too."

Mom smiled. "That sounds like a good idea."

Cody took the two packages of Goody Cakes and the George puppet and went outside. It had been awhile since he'd checked on the fort he and Quinn had made. He galloped over to the vacant lot behind the Kelleys' house. As he got closer, he could hear Quinn's voice.

"I'm going to dive off the high dive," she said in a pretend George voice.

In a Martha voice, she said, "Oh, you're so brave. It looks very high!"

She was rehearsing the play by herself! Cody crept closer.

"I'm not scared," she said again in the George voice. "Climb, climb, climb."

Cody was close enough to peek inside the fort. Quinn was using her stuffed monkey, Chi-Chi, to play the part of George. She had made a big blue wave that said Splash on it.

Cody stood there for a few seconds. Then he put the George puppet on his

hand. He stuck it around the edge of the fort. "Help me, Martha. It's scary up here," he said in his best George voice.

It got very quiet inside the fort. Cody swallowed hard. Still there was no answer. He pulled the George puppet back.

Just then, the Martha puppet peeked around the corner.

"Why should I help you?" she asked. "I thought you hated me."

"I don't hate you," he made the George puppet say. "It's just that Royce made me, I mean, Cody, so mad."

"Is that why Cody didn't tell about the cards?" asked Quinn-Martha. "Because he was mad at Royce?"

George's head nodded again. "To try to get even."

Martha smoothed her skirt. "Hmm."

Cody moved George closer. "How come you didn't tell?"

Martha tipped her head one way and then the other. "Even when friends say mean things, they're still your friends."

Cody sat back on his heels. Then he peeked around the corner himself. "Want to practice the whole thing?" he asked Quinn.

Her forehead crinkled. "Maybe," she said slowly.

Cody used his George voice. "I'll share my Goody Cakes with you," he said.

"What flavors?" asked Quinn.

"One package of chocolate, one of strawberry."

"I get the strawberry," she said.

"Okay," said Cody. "Do you want to practice first or eat Goody Cakes first?"

"What do you think?" Quinn asked.

Cody handed over the strawberry Goody Cakes.

CHAPTER TEN

"**W**e'll start our puppet shows right after lunch," said Mrs. Palmer at calendar time on Friday morning.

Cody turned to Quinn. *"Yess!"* he said.

"Ours will be the best," she said.

Cody thought so, too. They had practiced everything about a hundred times in the fort.

"Ours is going to be terrible," Annie May was telling Caitlin. "The puppet Royce made is so stupid looking."

Cody saw by the sad look on Royce's face that he had heard what Annie May said. He also saw a way that might fix Royce's Miss Nelson puppet and make it look better.

He picked up some yarn and some glue from the rainbow worktable. "I have an idea for your puppet," he told Royce.

"I don't need your help," said Royce.

"But if you twist the yarn like this for the hair and add some eyelashes—"

Royce pushed Cody away. "Just leave me alone," he said.

"Let's get ready for recess," Mrs. Palmer called.

Cody couldn't figure Royce out. Pure vinegar. He scurried over to get in the line.

He joined Jim and Josh in a game of spy-on-the-girls. They'd sneak over to the big tree, where the girls were playing pioneers, and then they'd jump out and scare them. The girls would scream—Annie May was the loudest—and run. It was a good game. Everyone was having fun. Until Royce came over.

He ran through the girls' camp and broke up their pretend house and campfire.

"Royce, you are a big pain." Annie May stamped her foot.

"Why don't you just go away?" asked Quinn. Brynn and Caitlin nodded. "Yeah!"

"I don't have to," said Royce. "Remember, Mrs. Moore says you can't lock anybody out from a game."

"That's for four square and wall ball," said Annie May.

"So what," said Royce.

Annie May gave Royce her mean look. "Why don't you play with your own friends?"

Royce blinked and jerked, like someone had thrown a ball at him and said think fast.

"Yeah, Royce. Play with your own friends," Caitlin echoed.

"He can't 'cause he doesn't have any," said Jim.

Royce's freckles lit up like glowworms.

"Royce hasn't got any fri-ends," Annie May singsonged. The other kids joined in.

"Shut up, Annie May." Royce moved toward her.

"I can say whatever I want." Annie May smirked. "It's a free country, isn't it?" She started singing again. "Royce hasn't got any fri-ends . . ."

Cody stepped back.

Royce was blinking faster now and swinging his fists around. But Cody could tell he didn't want to be vinegar anymore.

"Hey," Cody called out. "Let's play team tag!"

Annie May wrinkled her nose, but Quinn and Brynn grabbed hands. "Yeah!" they said. Team tag was even better than spy-on-the-girls.

"Me and Brynn are it first!" cried Quinn.

79

Caitlin screeched and ran one way with Annie May; Quinn and Brynn ran after them.

Jim and Josh danced around behind the big tree. "*Nyah, nyah,* you can't get us," they called.

"Yes, we can!" screamed Quinn and Brynn. But they turned and headed straight for Cody.

"Come on!" Cody ran over and tapped Royce on the shoulder. "Let's get out of here before they tag us!"

Royce stood there for a second with a peculiar look on his face.

"Hurry," said Cody.

Royce dropped his fists. "Okay!" He took off like a rocket car. Cody was right behind him. They didn't get tagged.

"Ready for some puppet shows?" Mrs. Palmer asked, after everyone was settled in the calendar corner.

Annie May and Royce went first.

Royce's Miss Nelson puppet looked much better since they'd added hair and eyelashes.

"Where's our teacher? Where's Miss Nelson?" Royce called from behind the puppet stage. Annie May had just the right voice for Viola Swamp.

"Very good," Mrs. Palmer said as the class clapped politely for Royce and Annie May. "Next?"

Cody and Quinn leaped up. "We are!"

Everything went perfectly. The whole class roared with laughter as the George puppet snuck down the ladder. The class clapped even louder than they had for Annie May and Royce, and Annie May had used her real puppet. The two puppets took a bow. The class kept clapping. Then, Quinn and Cody took a bow.

"You make a great team," said Mrs. Palmer. "That was lots of fun."

Cody and Quinn did high fives.

"Cody and Quinn," Royce's voice snaked

up from the back of the room, "sitting in a
tree . . ."

Mrs. Palmer looked over her shoulder.
"Oh, tick-a-lock, Royce," she said.

Even Royce laughed.

CHAPTER ELEVEN

"Cody, come on, we're going to miss the bus!" Quinn was pounding on the back door. Mom tossed Cody his lunch box.

When the bus came, Cody took the seat right behind Dora the Dragon Lady.

"Hey, Dora," Cody said, "how do bees go to school?"

Dora shook her head.

"They take the school *buzz!*" Cody giggled.

Dora the Dragon Lady laughed. Right out loud.

At school, Cody was daily helper. He picked Royce for a partner. They hurried to the office to pick up the bulletin and turn in the lunch count.

"Well, hi there, boys." Mrs. Moore waved to them from her office. "How's it going?"

Cody edged over toward the door. "Pretty good." Today, Mrs. Moore had a box of Chocobars on her desk. "I'm teaching Royce how to do waterfalls and freaky Fridays."

"I can already do a bird's nest," added Royce.

"That's great." Mrs. Moore smiled.

"Doing tricks on the bars is hard work. It takes a lot of energy," Cody said.

"It sure does. I remember that myself."

Cody looked at the box of Chocobars. Mrs. Moore put down her pencil. "Was there something else you boys wanted?"

Cody grinned. Royce grinned.

84

She gave them each a Chocobar. "Save these for after lunch," she said.

"Okay," said Royce.

"We promise," said Cody. They hurried back toward class.

Just outside Room three, Royce stopped and held out his Chocobar. "Hey," he said, "maybe you should have this."

"Why?" asked Cody.

"Just in case I do too many freaky Fridays," explained Royce. "Don't forget what happened to Brynn that time."

Royce tossed the Chocobar to Cody.

Cody caught it. Who would've thought? *Pow!*

go that far, but acceptance. Which is one fucking hell of a lot more than I'll ever get from Steener or Villanueva or anybody-the-fuck-else.

And Steener and Villanueva, they don't even get it, I know it just went right by them, what I told her. They'd do it because they're on the side of Good and Right.

I do it because I like to.

And I don't pretend like I ain't no monster, not for Good and Right, and not for Bad and Wrong. I know what I am, and the madwoman who put The Power and The Passion on my chest, she knew, too, and I think now she did it so the vamps would never get me, because God help you all if they had.

Just a coincidence, I guess, that it's my kind of picture.

Copyright Acknowledgments